THE SOCIETY FOR THE PROTECTION OF ENDANGERED AND AWESOMELY RARE SPECIES

For Logan
J.B.

For Barney,
who makes all things possible
A.L.

A special thanks to design whizz Jamie Hammond

First published 2020 by Walker Books Ltd
87 Vauxhall Walk, London SE11 5HJ

2 4 6 8 10 9 7 5 3 1

This book has been typeset in Arapey

Printed and bound in China

British Library Cataloguing in Publication Data: a catalogue record
for this book is available from the British Library

ISBN 978-1-4063-8845-9

www.walker.co.uk

WALKER
BOOKS

FSC
www.fsc.org
MIX
Paper from
responsible sources
FSC® C008047

AGENTS OF THE WILD

OF THE WILD

OPERATION HONEYHUNT

JENNIFER BELL & ALICE LICKENS

PROLOGUE

Agnes Gamble
could wait no longer. Eight years
was time enough to live without
a pet, especially for someone who loved
animals as much as her. She didn't mind
what kind of animal it was – furry or
scaly, winged or eight-legged – she just
wanted an animal to care for, a companion
that she could call her own.

For her birthday this year she was going
to ask – no, wait, DEMAND – that her
wishes be met. She wouldn't accept any
more excuses from her uncle Douglas.

"Pets devalue property," he always said.
"It's a simple fact."

"It's a simple fact that nothing else in the
world would make me happier!" Agnes would
tell him, before running up to her bedroom.

Douglas didn't understand her. How could he? He was an estate agent; all he knew about were property taxes, housing bubbles, off-street parking and something called stamp duty. Agnes's father had once told her that Douglas Brick wasn't even her proper uncle, but actually just her great-second-cousin-once-removed-and-two-put-back-again. Agnes liked to think of him simply as: all she had. It was easier that way.

In her bedroom, beside the scarce green-winged orchid she'd been trying to rehabilitate after a recent frost, there was a photo of Agnes's parents: Ranulph and Azalea Gamble.

"Not the famous botanists?!" I hear you cry.

Well, yes, actually. Those exact ones.

"The ones who were fatally crushed by

falling Bunya pine cones during a rare-flower-collecting trip to Australia?"

Indeed.

(Agnes was always surprised how many of the horrible details everyone seemed to know.)

Every time she looked at the photo of her parents, Agnes longed to be near them again; to hear the sound of her dad practising his rare-bird calls around the house; to smell the scent of her mum's orchid-and-frogspawn perfume in the hallway or to feel the press of their four arms around her, hugging her tight...

...But the wild had taken them; and now Agnes had been left in a big, grey city with nothing but a flourishing window box to remind her of who she really was.

CHAPTER ONE

It was on a sunny afternoon, on her way home from school, that Agnes took a detour through her favourite place in the city: the park. She'd been keeping an eye on a new family of squirrels who'd moved into the third sycamore along from the pond, and was becoming quite concerned.

"Maybe you should draw a map," she muttered, squatting down beneath an oak tree to gather fallen acorns. "Then you wouldn't forget where you'd stashed them."

A skinny little squirrel with cinnamon-coloured fur came scurrying down the trunk. Its eyes were wide and it was looking rather flustered. It stared at Agnes for a long moment before making a chirpy-squeak sound. Agnes knew it couldn't understand her, but she imagined it might be saying, "I'm a squirrel. I can't draw."

It was a good point. She sighed and placed the acorns in a bright green hand-kerchief, which she tied in a bow at the top.

Then she pulled her small "Field Notes" journal out of her top pocket – in which she recorded her observations about the natural world – and jotted down: *pencils for squirrels.* She'd add it to her list of "things to invent to make the world a better place".

"I'm leaving these here," she told the squirrel anyway, stretching up to the lowest branch of the tree and placing the handkerchief package on top. She fished a bicycle reflector out of her school bag (Uncle Douglas didn't ride his bike; he wouldn't miss it) and fastened it around the bark. "Just look out for the light; it should be easy to spot."

The squirrel flicked its tail and dashed up the tree. Agnes hoped that it would be curious enough to investigate her handkerchief and find the acorns inside.

As she turned back to the path, a pair of blacker-than-night eyes peeped out at her from the darkness of a nearby bush. They had been observing her very closely...

Blissfully unaware that someone was watching her, Agnes stopped by the pond and shielded the sun from her eyes as she looked out over the water. The resident Brecon Buff geese were swimming under the bridge, ruffling their pale brown feathers as they scooped leafy pondweed into their pink bills.

Agnes looked for the smallest goose in the flock. She usually found him sitting on his own on the bankside, nesting in a huff.

"Kenneth," Agnes called, cupping her hands around her mouth, "I've got your favourite!"

Suddenly, there was a splash and a loud honk and a small goose came charging across the water towards Agnes. The other geese noticed her too, and came swimming closer.

"There you are," Agnes said as Kenneth waddled up to her. He shut his deep brown eyes as Agnes stroked his soft head. She'd named him Kenneth because on the day she'd met him, he'd tried to eat her copy of *The Wind in the Willows* by Kenneth Grahame. Agnes hadn't been able to understand why he was so hungry at first – after all, there was plenty of bread around for all the geese to eat.

Determined to find out what was wrong, Agnes had searched through one of her parents' very large and very dusty books on common waterfowl and learned that bread wasn't really good for geese at all. It was like fast food; it filled geese up without giving them the nutrients they needed.

So now, Agnes reached into her pocket and retrieved a paper bag filled with her own special blend of oats, seeds, lentils and greens. She'd spent weeks perfecting the recipe to make sure it was extra tasty. "There's sunflower seeds in this batch," she said. "Here you go."

The blacker-than-night eyes watching Agnes blinked. *Incredible.* This little girl – with no proper training – had identified the dietary needs of a flock of geese and designed a feed mix to suit them.

Well, with those parents of course, was it any wonder? *What pedigree!* The girl obviously had special skills, skills that up until now had gone unnoticed by the rest of the world.

"I'm home!" Agnes shouted, returning to her twenty-sixth-floor flat.

"That's nice, Agnes," Uncle Douglas called to her from the kitchen. Agnes peered through the doorway at him. He was sitting at their dining table, hunched over his laptop, all attention focused on the screen. Behind him, Agnes noticed a pot of pasta about to over-boil on the stove, like always.

She shook her head and left Douglas to it, then trudged across the hall to her room. When she opened her door, she froze.

There was a *something* on her bed.

It was about the size of a large hamster, but it had a long tail and small ears and its body was covered in shiny fur that changed colour from fire-orange on its head, to jet black everywhere else. Its two blacker-than-night eyes were ringed in snow-white hair.

It blinked at Agnes and rolled onto its hind legs; and that's when Agnes noticed the most curious thing about it – it was wearing a tiny safari uniform: sand-beige, perfectly ironed and festooned with pockets.

"Er ... hello," Agnes managed, venturing slowly in and shutting the door quietly behind her. If Douglas saw she had an animal in her room, he'd go crazy. She took a deep breath, trying to control her shock. Studying the animal's features, she made an educated guess. "Are you a possum?"

The creature's arms flew to its hips as it puffed out its chest. "A POSSUM?" it exclaimed.

Agnes fell back against her bedroom door. The furry not-a-possum creature could speak? She didn't understand how it was possible... Was it some kind of trick? She stepped closer, her heart thudding like a train.

"I, *uneducated one,* am an ELEPHANT shrew, species *Rhynchocyon petersi.*"

Agnes stumbled to repeat the phrase. *"Rin-cho-sion..."*

"Never mind, girl. Never mind," the elephant shrew said. "There's no time for introductions." He pointed to a badge pinned to the lapel of his safari shirt. "I'm a field agent for **SPEARS**, and I need you to come with me, now."

CHAPTER TWO

"Don't dawdle, girl. We haven't got all evening." The elephant shrew stood tapping his little hairy foot against Agnes's bed, staring at her as she fiddled with the Velcro fastenings on a set of knee pads.

"What *are* these things?" she asked, adjusting one with a pinch of her fingers. They were covered in sticky green goo, which had already started dripping onto the carpet. The elephant shrew was wearing a matching pair, only smaller.

He rolled his dark eyes. "I *told* you. You really need to work on your memory skills. **SPEARS** technology is based on the science of the natural world. These knee pads are coated in a glue made from slug mucus. They'll help us stick to the walls as we climb up to the roof."

"You want me to scale the outside of this building?" Agnes exclaimed. "But we're twenty-six floors up! I'm a girl, not an Alpine goat."

The shrew sighed impatiently. "Not the *outside* walls, Miss Gamble." He hopped off

the bed and used his tail to slide aside a
mirror hanging beside Agnes's wardrobe.
Revealed behind it was a dark hole about
the size of a dustbin lid. "I took the liberty of
digging this passageway earlier using a Nile
crocodile burrowing spade. We'll be sticking
to the *inside* walls of the passage as we climb
up through the building."

"But why do we need to get to the roof?"

"To meet the **SPEARS** dragoncopter
that's waiting for us, of course," the shrew
answered. "We can't
exactly take the
stairs to reach
it – your uncle
would see. Oh,
and talking of
your uncle..."

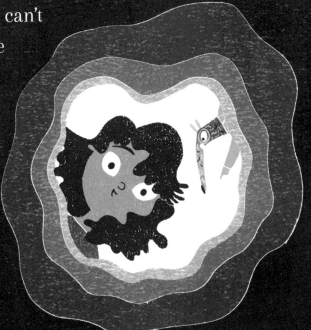

He knocked three times on the door of Agnes's wardrobe. *Tap. Tap. Tap.* It sounded like a secret code. All at once, the door sprang open and a chimpanzee dressed in a green corduroy dress, purple tights and a red wig stepped out.

"My clothes!" Agnes whispered, trying to keep her voice down. "What's going on?"

The chimp stood to attention and curled its huge pink lips together as if it was about to howl, but instead it cried: "My clothes!" in an identical voice to Agnes's. Then, with a very human-like gait, it walked over to Agnes's bed, sat cross-legged on top and began to read a book from her shelf, just like Agnes did every evening.

"This is Ralph," the elephant shrew explained. "He's been trained to mimic you, and to only be seen from behind.

When you're meant to be at home, your uncle will never know you're missing."

Agnes blinked, struck dumb with shock. "But ... he's a chimp."

The shrew nodded. "That is correct. Most children can be replaced for a short time with chimps, we've found."

Agnes's jaw dropped open. If it hadn't been for the stink of the slug mucus knee pads clinging to the back of her throat, she would have sworn she was dreaming. She thought about how her uncle Douglas would react if he walked into her room right now, to find a chimp in human clothing sitting on her bed, and an uppity little elephant shrew issuing instructions. She had to stop herself from bursting out laughing – it was just too bizarre to imagine.

"You still haven't explained why I need to come with you," she said. "I have no idea what **SPEARS** is, or how you can talk, or even what your name is."

The shrew cleared his throat and straightened up to his full height. "My name is *Rhynchocyon petersi*, as I clarified earlier."

"That's your species name," Agnes corrected. "People don't actually call you that."

The shrew ruffled his fur. "My friends call me Attenborough," he muttered. "Attie for short."

Agnes folded her arms. "Attie," she repeated, smiling. "Well, nice to meet you." She held out her hand – now covered in green goo.

Attie considered it with raised eyebrows. "I'm not here to make acquaintances."

He pointed proudly again to the pin badge on his safari shirt. Looking closer, Agnes could see it was designed with an animal-head logo in a circle. A tiny light seemed to be flashing in the centre.

"This communication pin is the reason I can talk to you. It uses lyrebird technology to help different species speak to each other. It's also the badge of **SPEARS**: the Society for the Protection of Endangered and Awesomely Rare Species."

"*Awesomely* rare?" Agnes frowned. "What makes something *awesomely* rare?"

Attie peered over his clipboard. "Let me see... Have you ever heard of the red-crested tree rat?"

Agnes turned to her bookshelves. Her father had given her a book called *Rodents*

of the World when she was
five. She'd read it over
and over but she couldn't
remember finding any kind
of red-crested tree rat inside. "Err ... no."

"Of course not; because they're
Awesomely Rare – that is, so rare in fact that
the majority of the human race don't even
know they exist. Most awesomely rare breeds
are critically endangered and in need of
SPEARS' help."

Agnes headed over to her bedside table,
where more photos of her mum and dad
looked out at her. "I don't understand. My
parents knew everything about the natural
world, and they never mentioned **SPEARS**
once to me."

Attie looked down at his hairy little feet.

"Yes, well, they were under strict instructions to keep **SPEARS** secret, even from you."

Agnes's eyes shot up. "My parents knew about **SPEARS**?!"

Attie nodded. "They were field agents, like me; though I never had the honour of working with them. Once they had you, they retired from **SPEARS** work. Thought it was too dangerous." He swallowed. "When **SPEARS** heard what had happened in Australia, everyone was devastated. We're very sorry..." His voice faltered.

Agnes sighed and looked deep into their faces in the photos. *SPEARS agents*; her parents? It sounded brave, dangerous and important – just the kind of thing they would have been involved in. They were the most courageous, smart and loving people she'd ever met.

She thought she'd known everything there was to know about them, but she'd been wrong. This was something new; and it felt amazing.

"And now you want *me* to come with you?" she asked, remembering what Attie had said.

The shrew nodded, although he looked less enthusiastic about the idea than he had done five minutes earlier. "Here, put these gloves on too. They're covered with the same slug mucus as the knee pads. I'll go first."

With a flick of his tail, Attie disappeared through the hole in the wall. Agnes poked her head inside. The passageway went straight up like the inside of a giant straw. She watched as Attie flattened himself against the smooth walls like a shrew-shaped rug. "You need a shimmying motion," he explained, shaking his body as if he was doing the samba. "Just copy me."

He looked ridiculous but Agnes was too nervous to laugh. Her stomach was doing somersaults as she put the climbing gloves on and crawled into the passage. Her hands and knees stuck to the surface of the walls like magnets, but as she climbed higher she didn't dare look down.

The thought of tracing her parents' footsteps filled her with determination. If she followed Attie, who knew what she might discover about them ... or herself. This was her chance to escape Uncle Douglas's dull, pet-free world and explore the one place that called to her more than any other: the wild. She swallowed and tilted her head, gazing up into darkness. Attie's tail was swinging to and fro as he wiggled forwards.

"Now follow me," he called, his voice echoing around the tunnel. "We don't have much time."

CHAPTER THREE

The **SPEARS** dragoncopter – a small, hovering aircraft able to make sudden sharp turns like a dragonfly – landed on the helipad of a skyscraper on the other side of the city. Agnes's ears were ringing from the noise of the rotary blades as she clambered out onto the tarmac, the wind battering her body.

"Keep your head down, Miss Gamble!" Attie instructed, heading towards a stairwell that led into the building. Agnes took one last look back at the dragoncopter – it was the first time she'd flown in anything – and, filled with new confidence, dashed after him.

"I know this place," she told him, noticing a cat-shaped logo on the side of the building. "It's the Fluffy-Face Cat Food Tower."

"We needed a cover-business to disguise who we really are," Attie explained. "It was either pet food or cookies." He stuck his tongue out, as if the thought of both foods made him feel sick. "There are a few big cats on the **SPEARS** board of trustees who pushed this through. I suggested fried bananas, but—"

"Fried bananas?" Agnes's brow crinkled as she closed the door behind them and the noise of the dragoncopter disappeared. "I've never heard of shrews eating fried bananas before."

"Not on their own of course," Attie clarified. "Pumpkin-seed-and-fried-banana sandwiches, however, are the staple diet of any shrew agent. Now stop asking questions; we're already late."

Attie led Agnes down a spiral staircase to a stainless-steel lift that played country music as it descended. Standing beside Agnes, Attie only reached Agnes's knee. He whistled happily and tapped his feet in time to the beat. Agnes decided to start a new page in her "Field Notes" journal to record her observations of him. She pictured him line-dancing, and wondered briefly if all shrew agents were into country music, or if Attie was just special. She'd never met an animal like him, and wanted to learn more.

A few floors down, the lift doors parted and Agnes lost her breath. Ahead of her was a brightly lit room, as wide across as a football pitch, with a high ceiling and polished floor. Humans and animals of all varieties were scurrying, trotting and flying around in every direction, carrying tablets and mobile phones. Some were wearing neat safari uniforms, like Attie, while others were dressed in diving gear, camouflage outfits or pilot suits. Agnes spotted them all wearing **SPEARS** communication pins attached to their clothes.

At the back of the floor stood a reception desk with a huge **SPEARS** logo mounted above it. A massive brown bear with black eyes was sitting behind the desk. Agnes made an assessment of the bear's features: *sharp claws, thick fur, over six feet tall... North American grizzly,* she decided.

Attie guided Agnes over and then stretched up on his tiptoes to peer over the desk. "Afternoon, Bluebell."

The bear's face broke into a smile, revealing a mouthful of off-white pointed teeth. "Oh, Attie," she purred in a soft voice, batting her eyelashes. Agnes noticed Attie's tail twitching.

Bluebell picked up a fluffy pink pen and ran it down a list on her desk. "Right on time, as always. The Commander can see you now. He postponed his meeting with those German investigators when he heard you were coming in with Miss Gamble." She pointed a claw towards a couple of stern-looking Alsatians in black suits who were sitting on dog cushions along from a large red door which had two human guards positioned outside. "They're here to talk about Axel Jabheart. He's been spotted again."

Attie scowled as they headed towards the guards. "Jabheart's an enemy of **SPEARS**," he explained to Agnes. "An illegal rare-insect collector."

Agnes shivered. "What's the Commander like?" she whispered, eager to change the subject.

"The Commander of **SPEARS** is the wisest, toughest and most fearless field agent we've ever had," Attie replied. "So remember your manners when we get inside. Not everyone gets a personal audience with him."

On the other side of the big red door was a luxurious office lined with mahogany bookcases. Antique globes and gleaming brass telescopes packed the shelves alongside books with titles like *On the Origin of Species* and *Moby-Dick*.

On the far side of the room was a huge desk, and behind it, a black chair with its back to them. Attie cleared his throat.

Agnes noticed his tail twitching again and wondered if he did it whenever he was nervous.

Slowly, the black chair rotated. Agnes didn't know who or what to expect to find sitting in it. If the **SPEARS** receptionist was a grizzly bear, she couldn't imagine what kind of dangerous animal might be their commander.

Agnes took a short breath as the chair came to a stop. A black wing lay on each armrest and between them was a plump feathered chest. His bald head was badly scarred and his wrinkled red neck was covered in tattoos. A pink fleshy snood hung from the top of his beak.

Agnes didn't need to list the Commander's identifying features to work out what creature he was. *Turkeys* were instantly recognizable.

"Excellent work, Attenborough," the Commander said in a hoarse voice, sending his snood wobbling. "**SPEARS** can always rely on you."

He got to his feet, his feathers fluffing out around the neck of his uniform like a Shakespearean ruff, and emerged from behind the desk. He had a canvas utility belt strapped round his waist packed with all kinds of tools and gadgets, most of which Agnes had never seen before. "Welcome to **SPEARS** HQ, Miss Gamble!"

"You're a turkey," Agnes said, quickly covering her mouth. She hadn't meant to say it aloud.

The Commander's throat wobbled. "Not what you were expecting, eh?" he said.

"You'll soon learn that at **SPEARS** every creature is valuable, be they man or mongoose." He held out a feathered arm. "Name's Phil."

Agnes shook Commander Phil's wing rather shamefacedly. She should have known not to judge someone on first appearances. The animal world was often full of deception and hidden secrets. It was one of the first things her parents had taught her.

"I hope Attenborough explained why we've  asked you here," he said, turning one of the antique globes on his shelves. "We are always on the lookout for talented new agents to help us do our crucial work. We've been keeping an eye on you for a while now and some of us have a hunch that you'll make a fantastic field agent, just like your parents."

"You want *me* to be a field agent?" Agnes asked, pointing to her chest. Her body felt numb with shock. She couldn't believe that was why they had brought her there.

"You'll have to go through training, of course, and then, when we think you're ready, you'll be sent on your first mission. If that's a success, you'll be invited to be a permanent field agent. What do you say?"

Agnes stared open-mouthed at Commander Phil, trying to find words. It felt like the world had stopped spinning and everything was happening in slow motion.

Attie nudged her in the knee, his jaw tight. "Well? Do. You. Accept?"

"I..." Agnes took a deep breath. The opportunity to follow in her parents' footsteps, to feel closer to them again and to continue their work helping vulnerable wildlife, was too important to turn away from, no matter how incredible it might be. "Yes," she said quietly. "Yes, I accept."

"Excellent!" Commander Phil threw his wings together in a soft clap and gave a gobbling laugh. "Training begins immediately."

CHAPTER FOUR

TRAINING IN PROGRESS

A red light flashed outside the door to the training room. "TRAINING IN PROGRESS," droned a robotic voice over the loudspeaker, "TRAINING IN PROGRESS."

Agnes smoothed down the **SPEARS** cargo jumpsuit that Attie had given her to change into. She could hear muffled shouts and thuds coming from behind the door and glanced down at Attie, wondering if she was about to regret saying yes to Commander Phil.

The red light went green. There was a loud click and then the door opened a fraction. Attie ushered Agnes inside.

They entered an enormous hall with padded walls and a ceiling fitted with spotlights. In the centre of the springy rubber floor was a silver climbing frame, the kind Agnes saw other children playing on in the park after school.

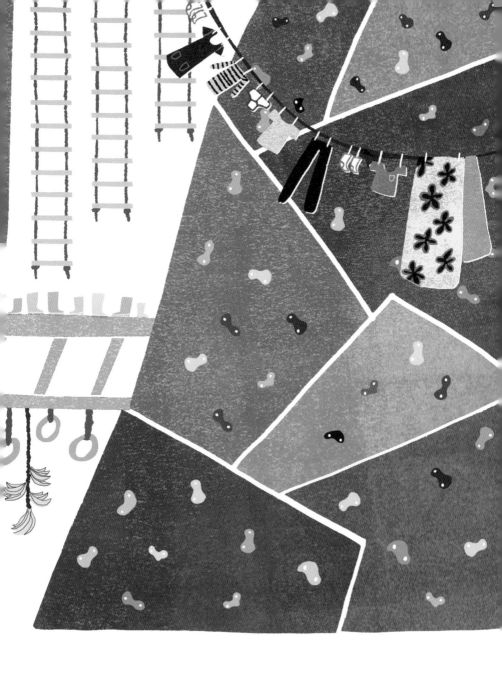

Rope ladders and chains hung down from the bars in various places, as did a bizarre assortment of other items – a large bunch of bananas, a pair of flowery bedroom curtains, several coconuts and a selection of wellington boots. A pool filled with floating logs and entangled seaweed lurked beneath one section of the frame.

Agnes started. She wasn't sure what she'd been expecting to find inside, but it wasn't this. She noticed red lights dancing across the toes of her **SPEARS**-branded trainers and tugged on Attie's sleeve. "What are those?"

"Sensors," he mumbled, brushing down the spot where she'd touched him. "They record all your performance data, so we can decide which field mission to send you on at the end."

Agnes swallowed. She had to get through training first.

As Attie marched her towards the centre of the hall, she spied three figures lurking in the shadows at different corners of the room. They all froze as Attie cleared his throat with a little squeak which echoed around the walls. "Agents, I'd like to introduce you to our new recruit, Agnes Gamble."

The figures began moving again very quickly. Agnes straightened herself up as Attie led her over to each of them in turn. First up was a tall hare with soft silvery-brown fur. It wore a khaki-green bandana tied around the base of its long ears, which flapped as it did a powerful combination of punches against a boxing bag suspended from the frame.

"This is Captain Marlena," Attie murmured to Agnes. "She's our resident expert in paw to paw combat. You'll learn the secret fighting-style of animai-tai from her. It's an agent's best form of self-defence, combining the combat skills of several different animals."

Agnes studied the black flecks in Captain Marlena's fur. *European brown hare*, she figured. They could run up to forty-five miles per hour and had powerful hind legs, which they used to "box" each other during mating season. No wonder she was their fight instructor.

Captain Marlena tilted her head, her focus fixed on the boxing bag. She squatted low and then leaped into the air, kicking with her long back legs. Agnes had seen videos of hares fighting before, but Captain Marlena's moves were different. They reminded Agnes of other animals doing battle. Captain Marlena performed a triple-loop kick through the air, snarling like a wolf, and then turned upside down, swinging like a monkey, before striking the boxing bag with such force it broke free of its chain and went hurtling into the climbing frame. A shower of bananas, coconuts and wellington boots hit the rubber floor and bounced off around the hall with the sound of a giant hailstorm.

Agnes fiddled
nervously with
the ends of
her sleeves as Captain
Marlena turned to her. "All
right there, kiddo? Looking forward
to your first lesson?" She had a
wonky smile and bright hazel eyes.

"Umm..." Agnes wasn't sure what to say.
"I don't know if I'll make a good fighter."

"Ah, you'll pick it up in no time," Captain
Marlena said, scuffing a paw through
Agnes's red hair. "I was as shy as a kit
when I started. All you need is agility,
strength and quick-thinking. We'll make a
first-class agent of you yet."

Agnes committed Captain Marlena's
advice to memory as she and Attie continued

towards another corner of the room, where an empty white chair was standing on the floor. As Agnes and Attie approached, the chair wobbled and – in one swift roll – suddenly changed into a large round bear with a white face and black patches over its eyes.

Agnes blinked. *A giant panda!* She had never seen one in real life before, only in her parents' photos. Giant pandas were a vulnerable species which normally inhabited the mountain ranges of central China.

The panda had a sleepy look on its face and a string of saliva hanging from its bottom lip as it chewed on a piece of bamboo. "The ... name ... is ... Shadowbelly," the panda said in a very slow, very soft voice. He continued munching while talking.

"I'll be … teaching you … the **SPEARS** techniques … of disguise. For some missions … you'll need to … go undercover or … hide from trouble."

Displayed on a long table beside him was a selection of props, including spectacles, a heap of dark green foliage, a pile of origami

paper, a paint palette and a large sombrero. In a black-and-white flash, Shadowbelly grabbed several items with his claws, threw half of them into the air and ruffled his thick fur. As the flying items landed back in his grasp, Agnes caught glimpses of him painting colours on his face, folding origami structures and stuffing leaves under his armpits.

In seconds, he had completely transformed into a tropical green plant with spiky purple and orange flowers. Agnes gasped. It was quite remarkable. In a muffled voice, Shadowbelly said, "Good agents ... always have ... a great deal of determination, patience ... and cunning. You'll need to ... demonstrate ... each of those ... to be successful."

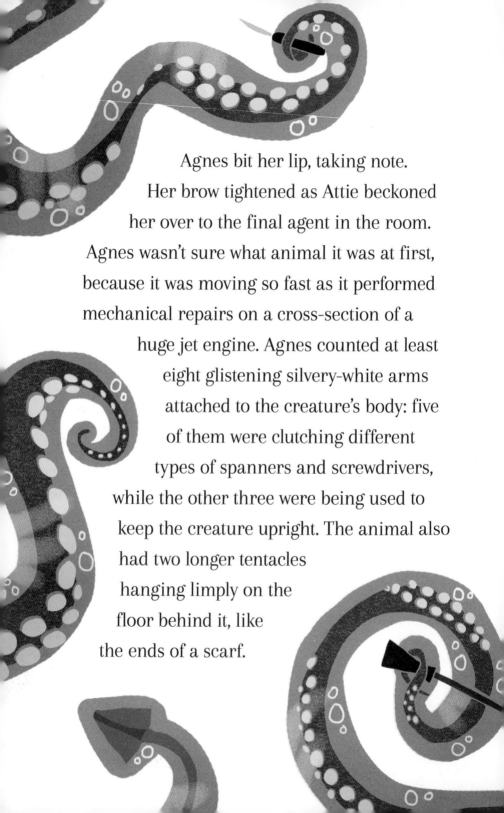

Agnes bit her lip, taking note.
Her brow tightened as Attie beckoned
her over to the final agent in the room.
Agnes wasn't sure what animal it was at first,
because it was moving so fast as it performed
mechanical repairs on a cross-section of a
huge jet engine. Agnes counted at least
eight glistening silvery-white arms
attached to the creature's body: five
of them were clutching different
types of spanners and screwdrivers,
while the other three were being used to
keep the creature upright. The animal also
had two longer tentacles
hanging limply on the
floor behind it, like
the ends of a scarf.

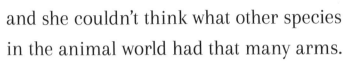

"Is the agent a squid?" Agnes whispered – she knew that octopuses didn't have the extra two tentacles and she couldn't think what other species in the animal world had that many arms.

Attie nodded, leaving Agnes to puzzle through how a squid could possibly survive out of water. As she approached, the agent stopped working and turned. Agnes saw that its entire body was covered in a transparent rubber suit filled with liquid; it looked like it was inside a balloon animal of itself. It had a triangular-shaped head with two watery black eyes and a wide smile that ran right across its face. It gave Attie a wobbly salute with one of its tentacles.

"Agnes, this is **SPEARS**' number one pilot and engineer, Aristophanes."

Agnes jerked her head. *"Pilot?* But squids live in the ocean."

"Ah, Miss Gamble," Aristophanes said. His voice seemed to come from a speaker attached to his special suit. "There is no creature better equipped to understand jet propulsion than a squid. It is how we swim underwater. I will be happy to teach you the basics this afternoon." He turned his head left to right. "I just need to find my star-head screwdriver..."

Agnes spotted the end of a long silver tool poking out from under one of the tentacles that he was using as a leg. She bent down and tugged it out. "Is this what you're looking for?"

"Aha!" Aristophanes exclaimed triumphantly. "I can see you'll make a fine agent – an eye for detail, imagination and courage. Those are essential. Now if you don't mind, I need to get back to work. I must finish this repair before your flight training."

As they headed back into the centre of the hall, Agnes ran through all the different qualities that the agents had told her she'd need to demonstrate to make a good **SPEARS** agent. The list made her stomach tighten. Her parents had possessed each of them for sure, but she had none of their experience or knowledge – how could she? All she did was go to school and live with her uncle Douglas. She wondered briefly how he was getting on with her chimp replacement.

The afternoon passed quickly. First, Agnes learnt the basics of animai-tai with Captain Marlena. Agnes's reflexes were surprisingly good; perhaps all that time spent dodging angry geese and trying to avoid stepping on squirrel tails had helped. She realized she was a lot stronger than she thought too – then again, she'd never done a flying-hyena-lightning-strike attack on a punchbag before, so she had little to compare it to.

Shadowbelly taught her two elementary-level disguises: the sandy bank and the jungle tree trunk. Each required Agnes to learn and refine a series of steps to create the overall camouflage. It was all about speed and precision.

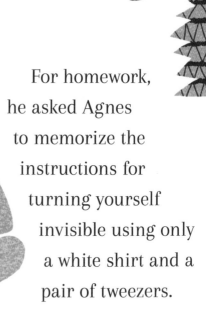

For homework, he asked Agnes to memorize the instructions for turning yourself invisible using only a white shirt and a pair of tweezers.

Under Aristophanes' instruction, Agnes did an hour's worth of flight simulation, focusing on the role of co-pilot.

Afterwards, Attie went through some essentials from the **SPEARS** training manuals, which were written in several languages, including two types of Baboon-speak. The chapter on "How to Calm Saltwater Crocodiles" was particularly illuminating.

Attie also gave her a **SPEARS** communication pin so she could talk to – and understand – other creatures from the animal kingdom. He finished by directing Agnes to the food preparation unit and giving her lessons in making pumpkin-seed-and-fried-banana sandwiches. "If we're to work together, it's essential that you master this recipe," he said, every time she slathered on a little too much mixture. "I can't survive on anything less."

The next day, Agnes made pumpkin-seed-and-fried-banana sandwiches for breakfast, just to practise.

She returned to the training room at **SPEARS** HQ every weekday for a month. Uncle Douglas didn't even seem to notice that she fell into bed each evening exhausted by the extra study and exercise. Her ribs hurt from all the stretching and fighting she'd do with Captain Marlena and her eyes ached from concentrating so hard in the flight simulator. But her longing to be a field agent drove her on and, as her body grew stronger, her confidence increased.

Finally, the day came when Attie tapped her on the shoulder. "That's all for now. You've made good progress. The agents have decided that you're ready."

Agnes tingled with anticipation. *Ready for what?* She took a deep breath and pushed her shoulders back as Commander Phil called them into the briefing room.

Attie took a seat in the front row. Agnes sat beside him with Captain Marlena, Aristophanes and Shadowbelly behind.

"We've analysed your training scores,

Miss Gamble," Commander Phil said, fluffing up his black chest feathers, "and we're very pleased. We think you're ready to move on to the next stage of your training: in the field. You've been assigned your first mission, after which we'll decide if you've got what it takes to be a permanent **SPEARS** agent." He pointed over his shoulder to a strange typewriter surrounded by pink smoke, out of which was printing a long reel of paper.

MISSION NAME: OPERATION HONEYHUNT
MISSION TYPE: Rescue and relocate
SPECIES NAME: Uruçu negra (common)
Melipona capixaba (scientific)
ASSIGNED EQUIPMENT: Eco-fuel albatross glider, raindrop refractor, animapper

Commander Phil cleared his throat. "As we all know, deforestation is destroying the habitats of many creatures who live in rainforests. Last week, **SPEARS** was tasked with relocating a hive of endangered *uruçu negra* bees in the Atlantic Forest to a protected sanctuary two hundred kilometres away. These bees do an important job pollinating many of the rare plant species in the area and are a vital part of the ecosystem. Sadly, an unexpected thunderstorm caused complications during the operation. In a rush to leave, the queen bee made a miscalculation when counting the colony and ... one bee was left behind."

Behind Agnes, the other agents gasped.

"This missing bee is only a youngster," Commander Phil continued. "He's bound to be lost and disorientated and, to make matters worse, Axel Jabheart has been sighted in the Atlantic Forest in the last two days, so the missing bee is at even greater risk.

"Agnes and Attie – you must rescue the bee and return him safely to his hive at the **SPEARS** sanctuary. You'll set off first thing tomorrow, taking the mid-Atlantic flight route. Be careful. There will be many hazards in the jungle, and communication with HQ may be difficult."

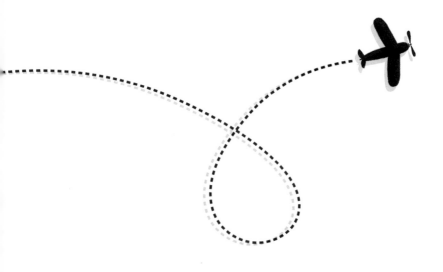

CHAPTER FIVE

"Crrrr...Crrrr..."

Agnes stuck her head out of the albatross glider window and shouted as loud as she could, "Attie, we've lost the video feed again!" She hoped he could hear her above the roar of the wind. A rainstorm over the South Atlantic Ocean had damaged their external navigation equipment, so Attie had been forced to strap himself to the roof of the glider in order to guide them in.

The air was hot and sticky. Agnes adjusted her flight goggles as they glided lower across the lush green rainforest. Rivers snaked between the densely packed treetops and flocks of brightly coloured parrots flitted from one tree to another. Agnes spotted the striking turquoise plumage of a seven-coloured tanager bird hopping between branches. Her skin tingled as she thought of all the strange and wonderful creatures that called this place home.

"*Crrr... Crrr...* Agent Gamble? Can you hear me?"

Agnes turned back to the cockpit as the image on the video screen returned. An orange-beaked macaroni penguin sat typing at a keyboard with his flippers. The operations room at **SPEARS** HQ buzzed with activity in the background. "I've hacked the glider's flight controls," the penguin said. "I can pilot you in, but I'll be flying blind; you'll need to co-pilot using Attie's directions. *Crrr... Crrr...*"

The screen crackled and the image disappeared again. Agnes swallowed and grabbed the yoke – a small wheel that controlled the altitude of the glider. Her hands were shaking.

Attie shouted from the wings, "There's a clearing on the right heading zero three zero. Descend to one thousand feet."

She tried to remember what Aristophanes
had taught her in the flight simulator, as
she steered the glider lower, banking to
the right.

"Now, prepare for landing!"
Attie cried. Branches snapped and
crunched as the wings of the glider
clattered through the forest canopy.
"Keep her steady; we're almost there."

A curtain of vines fell onto the glider's nose, tangling in the propeller blades, and with a loud, sputtering noise, the engine choked out. "Hold on!" Agnes's grip tightened as the aircraft plunged the last few metres to the ground and landed with a jerk amongst the roots of a large tree with spiky seed pods.

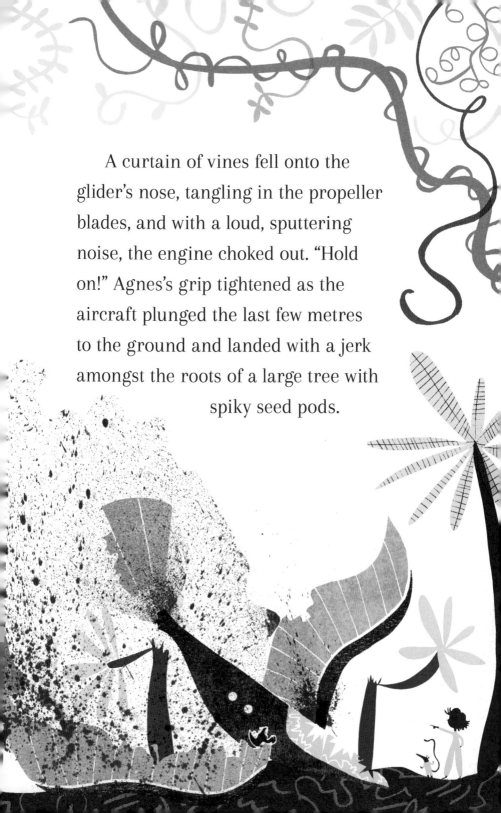

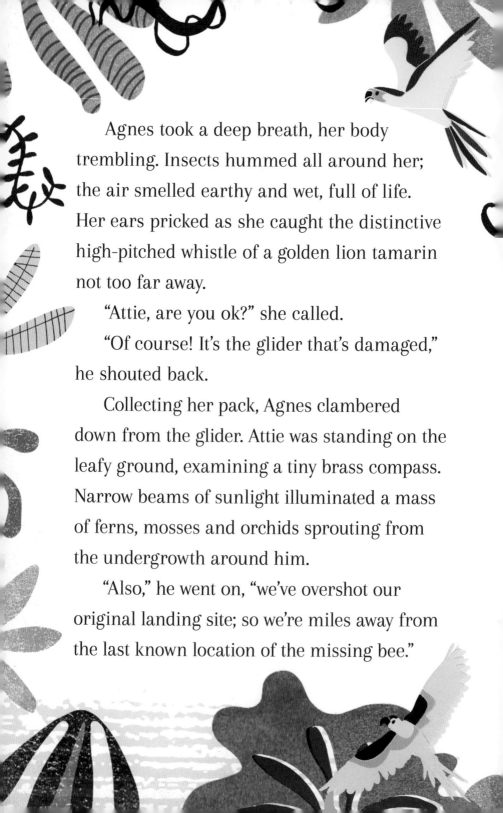

Agnes took a deep breath, her body trembling. Insects hummed all around her; the air smelled earthy and wet, full of life. Her ears pricked as she caught the distinctive high-pitched whistle of a golden lion tamarin not too far away.

"Attie, are you ok?" she called.

"Of course! It's the glider that's damaged," he shouted back.

Collecting her pack, Agnes clambered down from the glider. Attie was standing on the leafy ground, examining a tiny brass compass. Narrow beams of sunlight illuminated a mass of ferns, mosses and orchids sprouting from the undergrowth around him.

"Also," he went on, "we've overshot our original landing site; so we're miles away from the last known location of the missing bee."

Agnes's heart sank but she tried to remain focused. Her parents wouldn't have let a problem like this faze them on one of their **SPEARS** missions. "We need to look for clues. There must be evidence of the missing bee somewhere." She took a seat on the enormous buttress roots of a guapuruvu tree and read back through the mission briefing Commander Phil had given them.

"It says here that bees communicate by buzzing," she told Attie. "Perhaps we should check if the missing bee is sending out a distress signal?"

Inspecting the propeller blades, Attie nodded. "Good idea, but it'll be difficult to hear a bee in all this racket. Try using this animapper." He took what looked like a small silver radio out of his backpack and tossed it to Agnes. "It works using bat echolocation, listening for nearby sounds to draw a map of the area. You have to adjust the frequency until you find the correct animal sound that you're looking for."

The animapper had a video screen on the front and a dial on one side. Agnes turned the dial until it clicked and the screen lit up, showing an outline of the surrounding forest. The speaker crackled and emitted a low *woop*, followed by a long *eee-ooo*. Agnes recognized the noise instantly. She'd played rare-bird call hide-and-seek with her parents enough times to know: it was the cry of a red-billed curassow – a large ground-foraging bird with glossy black feathers. The bird's location appeared on the animapper screen, but Agnes ignored it and turned the dial again.

Next, she heard the distinctive howl of a woolly spider monkey and then the croak of a red-eyed tree frog. Neither of those were any help. Adjusting the dial one click at a time, she listened carefully to each animal noise that followed, searching for the missing bee.

Over an hour had passed when she felt something furry tap her on the knee. "Don't give up, Agent Gamble," Attie said, smiling up at her. "It takes a lot of patience to operate an animapper; you're doing well."

Although Agnes appreciated the vote of confidence, her shoulders sagged. "But I still haven't located the *uruçu negra* bee and we're running out of time."

"Let's look at the problem from a different angle." Attie scrunched up his long nose, thinking. "Have you tried switching on your

SPEARS communication pin?"

Of course. Agnes brightened and did as Attie had suggested. When she next clicked the dial on the animapper, rather than animal noises she heard two very slow voices.

"Look at him ... over there," said the first, sleepily. "He's all by himself."

"I wonder if ... his colony are ... looking for him," commented the second with a yawn.

"I'm sure ... they are," the first replied. "Every ... bee is ... important to ... a hive."

"Attie, did you hear that?" Agnes said, her hands shaking. "I think they're talking about our missing bee!"

Attie checked the screen on the animapper. "They're this way – come on!"

They hurried through the jungle in the direction of the two mystery creatures

and finally came to a small clearing.
There, hanging from the branches of
another guapuruvu tree were two shaggy-
haired animals with long limbs, round
heads and flat faces. Agnes identified them
easily: a pair of maned three-toed sloths. No
wonder they'd been speaking so slowly; they
were among the slowest creatures in the
animal kingdom.

"Excuse me!" Agnes called, waving up to
them. "We're looking for a lost bee. Can you
help us?"

As the sloths began to slowly turn their heads, Attie dragged a paw down his face, groaning. "We really don't have time for this."

In three quick jumps he bounded up the guapuruvu tree trunk to where the sloths were hanging and, after pointing to his **SPEARS** badge, asked them several urgent questions. Agnes watched with interest as the sloths eventually signalled to a small green leaf near the forest floor.

Wasting no time, she hurried over and inspected it carefully. Flopped on top was a single black bee the size of her little finger-nail. She gasped. "Attie, we've found him!"

"Excellent!" Attie said, hopping down to join her. "Now, stand back. I need to fit the bee with a communication pin and a raindrop refractor belt so we can check if he's injured."

Agnes had no idea what a raindrop refractor belt was, but she gave Attie space as he set to work. A moment later, a larger-than-life hologram of the bee flickered into life right above where he was lying.

Now the size of a puppy, the bee could be viewed in perfect detail. His chubby face, large round body and even larger bottom were covered in velvety black fur which

sparkled with little flecks of gold. Covering
his eyes was a pair of star-shaped sunglasses
with lenses the colour of tree sap. A blue belt
with the **SPEARS** logo hung loosely around
his tummy: the raindrop refractor.

"Hello?" the bee asked, looking between
Agnes and Attie, his antennae twitching.
"Who are you? And why do I feel so big?"

"Don't be scared," Agnes said in a soft
voice, stepping forward. "My name's Agnes

and this is Attie. We're **SPEARS** agents.
We're here to help you. We're using a special
gadget to make you appear bigger so we can
see you better."

The bee hesitated for a moment, and
then fluttered its wings excitedly. "Nice to
meet you, Agnes and Attie! I'm Elton." As he
shuffled over the leaf, Agnes noticed that one
of his six black legs was hanging limply.

"Careful," she said, "you're hurt."

Elton's antennae drooped. "Yes, it
happened when I crash-landed during a
thunderstorm. I think it's broken. I can't fly
any higher than this, it's too painful."

"Don't worry." Attie jumped forward,
holding a tape-measure to Elton's hologram
leg. "I'll have a splint fashioned for that in a
jiffy. In the meantime, we should make camp."

He squinted up through the forest canopy. "The light is fading. It'll be tomorrow morning before I can repair the glider to get us out of here."

"A splint? For *me?*" Elton's fur shivered. "I've never had a splint before. Will it be stylish? Perhaps we could use *ruffles*?"

"We *do not* use ruffles at **SPEARS**," Attie said sharply.

Agnes noticed Elton's antennae droop. She gave Attie a hard stare.

"What I *meant* to say," Attie quickly corrected, "is that we don't *usually* make splints with ruffles because they don't work as well. And we wouldn't want that."

"No." Elton shrugged. "I guess you're right."

Agnes gave Elton a smile and pointed to the badge on her uniform. "**SPEARS** is the

Society for the Protection of Endangered and Awesomely Rare Species," she explained.

"You were the people helping my colony to move hive, weren't you?" Elton said. "Do you know if they're all right? They ... they left without me." His wings went still and he flopped down onto the surface of the leaf. "I was out pollinating when the storm hit. I tried to get back to the hive in time for the move, but after I injured my leg I couldn't fly fast enough." He sniffed. "I miss my colony so much. I don't understand why they forgot about me."

Agnes squatted down so she was at Elton's level. Very gently, she extended her little finger and stroked Elton's soft black fur. "They didn't forget about you. Your queen made a mistake and thought every bee had

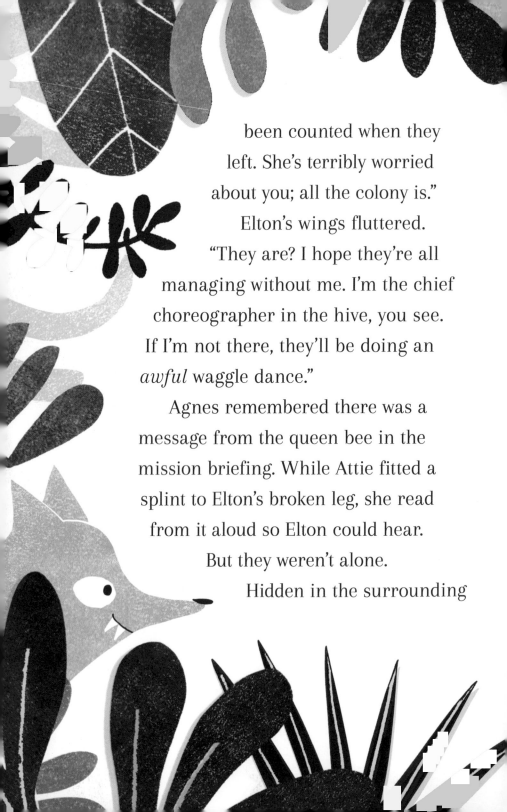

been counted when they left. She's terribly worried about you; all the colony is."

Elton's wings fluttered.

"They are? I hope they're all managing without me. I'm the chief choreographer in the hive, you see. If I'm not there, they'll be doing an *awful* waggle dance."

Agnes remembered there was a message from the queen bee in the mission briefing. While Attie fitted a splint to Elton's broken leg, she read from it aloud so Elton could hear.

But they weren't alone.

Hidden in the surrounding

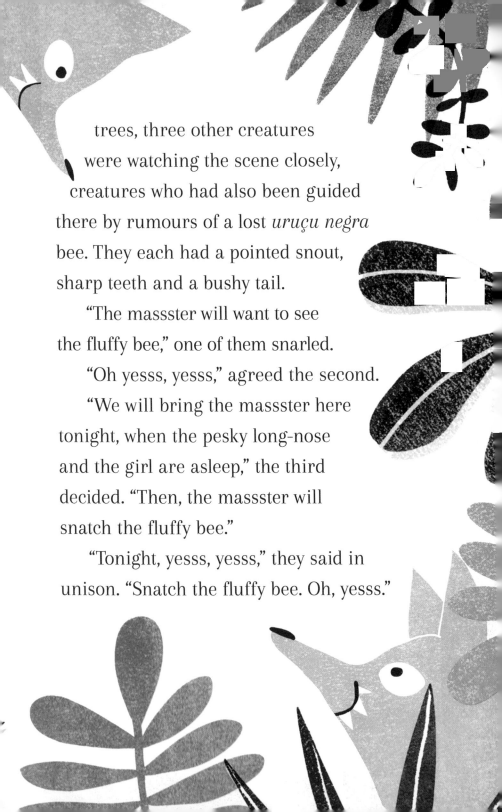

trees, three other creatures
were watching the scene closely,
creatures who had also been guided
there by rumours of a lost *uruçu negra*
bee. They each had a pointed snout,
sharp teeth and a bushy tail.

"The massster will want to see
the fluffy bee," one of them snarled.

"Oh yesss, yesss," agreed the second.

"We will bring the massster here
tonight, when the pesky long-nose
and the girl are asleep," the third
decided. "Then, the massster will
snatch the fluffy bee."

"Tonight, yesss, yesss," they said in
unison. "Snatch the fluffy bee. Oh, yesss."

CHAPTER SIX

Sitting with her back against a large
Brazilian rosewood tree, Agnes took out her
"Field Notes" journal and began to write...

OPERATION HONEYHUNT

by Agnes Gamble (schoolgirl and trainee agent for **SPEARS**)

UPDATE:

After successfully locating the missing *uruçu negra* bee, we have set up camp in the jungle. Agent Attenborough plans to fix the albatross glider at first light tomorrow. It is incredibly dark and noisy, but Agent Attenborough has lit a fire and now the rescued bee (who goes by the name of Elton) is asleep. I am on first watch.

OBSERVATIONS:

ELTON (*Melipona capixaba*)
LIKES: Ruffles, music and dancing. Favourite food is pollen popcorn. Favourite song is "All the Single Bees" by Bee-yoncé.

DISLIKES: Being alone. Seems to get shy around other animals.

NOTES: Elton has dense, fluffy black fur in which he stores several pairs of novelty sunglasses, which he changes at least once every hour. He is a brilliant dancer, and even moves his legs in time to a beat when asleep.

ATTIE (*Rhynchocyon petersi*)

LIKES: Pumpkin-seed-and-fried-banana sandwiches. Bluebell, the grizzly bear who works at **SPEARS** Headquarters.

DISLIKES: Human girls, dancing, ruffles, being stroked.

NOTES: Attie is very brave. He is skilled in lots of things, from mechanics and flight control, to first aid and engineering. He appears to like all animals, except human girls ... although when he thinks I'm not looking, I've seen him glance at me and smile.

OTHER:

* During short expeditions into the surrounding jungle I have spotted passion-fruit vines, Venus flytraps, orchids, giant water-lilies and rubber trees.
* The nearest freshwater source is a narrow river filled with huge arapaima fish that breach the surface to gulp in air, and schools of red-bellied piranhas.
* A family of poison dart frogs (species *Dendrobates tinctorius*) are living in a tree just outside camp. I have been careful not to touch them, as the poison secreted from their skin can cause itchiness and burning.
* The droppings of several species of monkey cover the jungle floor.
* I have collected leaf samples from: a bird's-nest fern and a cacao tree.

Three small creatures with snow-white fur and tiny black noses padded slowly across the jungle floor. Sweat ran off their backs, their tongues lolling out of their mouths.

"This place isss too hot," complained one of them. "We can't think straight."

"But the massster has ice cream," growled another, flicking aside a branch with its tail.

"Ice cream, yesss," agreed the third. "That will cool usss down. When we tell Massster about the bee who isss fat, then we will get the ice cream."

They entered a flood-lit clearing. A black four-by-four was parked in the centre, beside a large net enclosure.

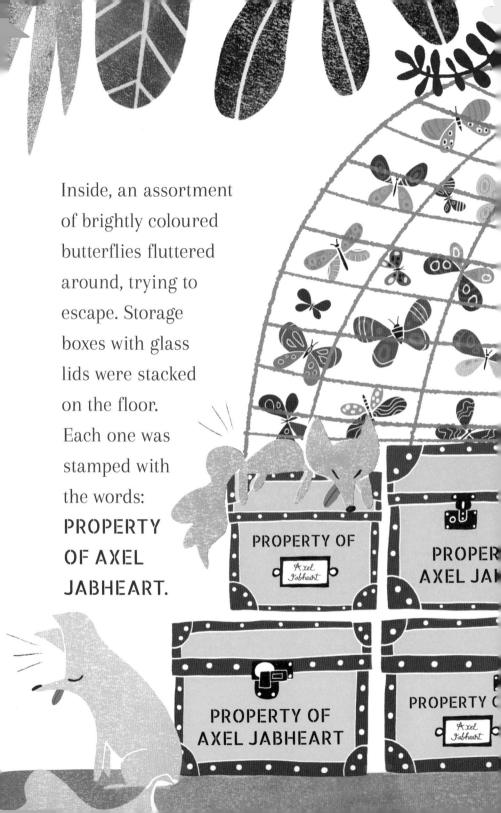

Inside, an assortment of brightly coloured butterflies fluttered around, trying to escape. Storage boxes with glass lids were stacked on the floor. Each one was stamped with the words: **PROPERTY OF AXEL JABHEART.**

PROPERTY OF

Axel Jabheart

PROPER
AXEL JA

PROPERTY OF
AXEL JABHEART

PROPERTY O

Axel Jabheart

A tall man in a slim-fitting silver suit stood cleaning one of the storage boxes. His white-blond hair was styled into a Mr Whippy-shaped swirl, and he had glacier-blue eyes and ice-white skin, as if he'd spent his life in a freezer.

"What are you three doing back?" he snapped. "I told you to stand guard all night." He continued rubbing a cloth across one of the boxes. "I do not like to be disturbed when I am polishing." The jewelled bodies of dead beetles glittered beneath the glass. They had been pinned with their wings open, and labelled in scratchy handwriting.

"But we have information, Massster Jabheart," one of the creatures said, panting.

PROPERTY O

Axel
Jabheart

PROPERTY
AXEL JABHE

"It's just that we can't think in this heat, Massster. We're Arctic foxes; we're not adapted for these temperatures."

Axel Jabheart laughed bitterly. "You're not adapted to water either, but that didn't stop you taking a snorkelling holiday with your last pay cheque, did it?"

The Arctic foxes shared embarrassed glances.

Jabheart's eyes narrowed. "*What information?*"

"We found something you're going to want to ... pin down for your collection," one fox said.

"My collection?" Jabheart stroked his curled moustache. "Go on..."

"Yesss, Massster, a bee who isss fluffy. Fluffy and black with shiny wings."

"A fluffy black bee you say..." Jabheart

ran a finger across another of the insect cases. "Did its fur look like soft black velvet with golden flecks?"

"Exactly like that, Massster," the foxes answered in unison.

Jabheart froze. "What?" The foxes grinned as he stepped closer, lowering his head to their short muzzles. "This bee ... was it *wearing sunglasses*?"

The foxes nodded furiously.

Axel Jabheart swayed side to side, a delirious smile filling his face. "I don't believe it!" He grabbed the foxes and threw them into the air as if they were no heavier than confetti. "It's an *uruçu negra* bee, boys! And the choreographer of the hive, if it's wearing sunglasses! They're extremely rare in the wild and only found in this part of the Atlantic Forest."

He rubbed his chin as the foxes crashed to the ground. "If I capture one, people will come from all over the world to see it displayed behind glass in my collection. It would be the crowning triumph of my life's work! Where is the insect now?"

The foxes coughed as they got to their feet. "Perhaps ice cream would help usss remember better in this heat, Massster?" they said as one.

"*Ice cream?!* Is that all you mange-balls ever think about?" Jabheart opened the boot of his four-by-four and retrieved a tub of chocolate-chip ice cream. "Now listen carefully: *where is the* uruçu negra *bee*?"

The Arctic foxes stared at the ice-cream tub. "Not too far away. We will show you. The bee is with **SPEARS** agents. They have made a camp."

"**SPEARS**!?" Jabheart threw the tub down in a rage. As it split open, the Arctic foxes pounced on it and started licking. "That confounded organization is always getting in my way. If it wasn't for them, I would have got my hands on that red-fanged funnel spider last summer." He paused. "Maybe if we take them by surprise we can snatch the bee right out from under their noses. But only if we strike now."

"Now?" One of the foxes looked up, melted ice cream smeared over its muzzle. "Right now?"

"Yes, right now," Jabheart retorted. "Or would you like me to start collecting specimens of Arctic mammal instead?"

CHAPTER SEVEN

Agnes yawned and stretched her arms. The jungle was filled with so many loud noises it should have been easy to stay awake and keep watch, but she was exhausted. She glanced over her shoulder, checking on camp. Attie was curled up in a ball on the floor, snoring. Elton, still wearing his raindrop refractor belt, was sleeping in a miniature leaf-hammock that Attie had constructed.

As Agnes looked back round, she saw something padding through the trees. It was small – about the size of a dog – with four legs, pointed ears and snow-white fur.

She rubbed her eyes, wondering if she was seeing things. There weren't any white-furred animals in the Atlantic Forest that she knew of. Getting to her feet and slinging her pack over her shoulder, she headed off to investigate.

The mystery creature was fast but Agnes was careful to stay out of sight. When she was close enough, she switched on her torch.

As the light fell across the creature's bushy tail and short snout, Agnes went stiff with shock. Its features were so distinctive.

An Arctic fox?

But ... she didn't understand. They lived in the Arctic regions of the northern hemisphere, not the jungles of South America.

Before she could learn more, there came a loud *WHOOSH* and a sudden *SNAP* from back at camp.

The Arctic fox pricked
up its ears and, with a flick
of its tail, disappeared
into the trees.

Agnes heard Attie shouting. Her
heart pounded as she raced back through the
jungle to camp. As she drew closer, she slowed.
A voice she didn't recognize was talking...

"Hoist him up, boys. We don't want the little rodent getting away."

Rodent...? Agnes hid behind a giant jungle fern and peeked through the leaves to see what was going on.

She gasped when she saw that Attie was trapped in a net, hanging from a tree. Tugging on the ends of the hoisting ropes were two Arctic foxes. A third fox was dangling a glittery gold-and-pink disco ball in front of Elton, who had frozen stiff with his eyes fixed like he'd been hypnotized. A thin man in a dazzling silver suit with a white quiff of hair stood by the side, looking rather smug.

"You won't get away with this, Jabheart!" Attie shouted, wriggling his long nose through a hole in the net. "**SPEARS** has

stopped you before and it will again! Even as I speak other **SPEARS** agents are on their way here to rescue me."

Jabheart laughed. "Perhaps, but that bee and I will be long gone before they arrive."

Agnes knew that Attie was bluffing. They had lost communication with **SPEARS** HQ on the flight in. The only person who could possibly save Attie and Elton now was ... *her*.

She swallowed, trying not to panic. Her parents had probably found themselves in tricky situations just like this when they were **SPEARS** agents. She couldn't fail now.

First, I need my partner back.

Remembering her time with Agent Shadowbelly, she pulled her disguise-kit out of her pack and quickly got to work fashioning one of the costumes that she'd practised in training. A minute later, a remarkably authentic-looking pau-brasil tree trunk shimmied into camp. The leaves covering Agnes's body rustled loudly so she moved in short bursts, keeping a close eye on Jabheart and the Arctic foxes.

"Leave the bee alone!" Attie demanded as Agnes came closer. "What have you done to him?"

Jabheart smiled wickedly. "Impressive trick, isn't it? My studies have shown that most dancing insects have a doomed attraction to disco balls. If they stare at one for too long, it sends them into a trance. The bee has been bamboozled."

Poor Elton. Agnes couldn't bear it. She positioned herself close to one of the Arctic foxes who was holding the ropes to Attie's net

and slipped her hand out of her costume. In it was the sample of bird's-nest fern that she'd collected earlier. It had extremely soft and ticklish leaves. Very carefully, she waved it under the fox's belly.

At first, the fox twitched.

Then it stamped its feet.

Then it began hopping around madly. "Ahh!" it cried through gritted teeth. "Ssstop the tickles, the tickles!" With one great yelp, it released the rope from its jaws and the net fell open.

Attie dropped to the ground in a crouch and quickly sprang to his feet, looking around. "Agent Gamble, are you there?"

Agnes shook off her tree-trunk camouflage, giving the Arctic foxes a shock.

"Excellent," Attie declared. "You free Elton while I deal with Jabheart."

Agnes nodded, though she wasn't
sure how she was going to get past the Arctic
foxes. As two of them stalked towards her,
she remembered something Captain Marlena
had taught her during her animai-tai lesson:
*if you find yourself outnumbered, use your
environment to defend yourself.*

Agnes thought of the field notes she'd made
earlier – about the plants and animals in the
surrounding jungle. They gave her an idea.

"Catch me if you can, Hairballs!" she
called, running into the trees. The Arctic
foxes set off in pursuit.

Pulling on a pair of **SPEARS**-branded
gloves, Agnes shot straight for the tree she'd
seen covered in poison dart frogs. "I'm very
sorry about this," she told the frogs as she

drew closer, "but it's an emergency. I desperately need some of your poison."

The largest frog croaked angrily at her.

"Please, I'm on a mission with **SPEARS**." She pointed to the logo on her communication pin. "You've got to help me."

The large frog considered her carefully and then rolled onto its back. Agnes sagged with relief. "Thank you."

Very gently, she rubbed several leaves across the frog's tummy and then placed them on the floor, poison-side up. She was finished not a moment too soon, as two Arctic foxes emerged through the trees.

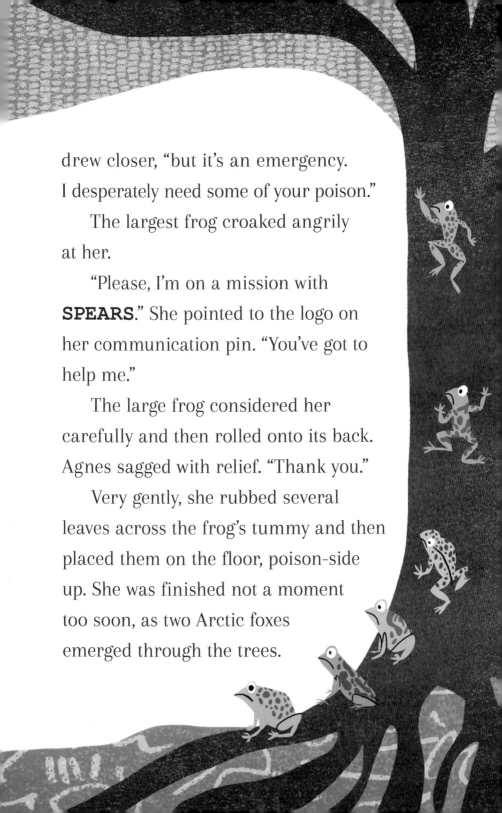

"I'm over here!" Agnes taunted, pulling faces at them.

The first Arctic fox bounded towards her with its jaw hanging open. Stepping on the poisoned leaves, it frowned and skidded to a halt.

"Argh, it burnsss!" it yelped, hopping from paw to paw as if the forest floor was on fire. "Hot! Hot!"

The second Arctic fox narrowed its gaze on Agnes and trod *around* the poisoned leaves.

Agnes's nerves tightened.

This fox appeared to be smarter
than the other one; it would be difficult
to outwit. Knowing she had to move, she
turned and ran, heading for the river.

The trees on either bank were
covered in passion-flower vines,
heavy with dark purple fruit.
Agnes tugged at one of the
branches and found it was
strong enough to take her
weight, so she began
climbing.

Using the iron-sloth-grip technique that Captain Marlena had taught her, she secured herself in the jungle canopy and shone her torch into the water below.

The current was fast but she could still make out the golden scales of red-bellied piranhas, glittering in the depths. She switched the light off; in the darkness it was difficult to see the water's edge.

"I've got you now," the Arctic fox said, appearing in the undergrowth. It grinned as it crept towards her. "Jussst stay *right* there."

It reared on its hind legs and leapt for Agnes, but she was too fast. Performing a flaming-toucan-swoop, she catapulted into the treetops, out of the way. The fox missed her and fell into the river with a huge splash.

"Pesssky bitey fish!" it growled as the water swirled with bubbles around it. "Get off!"

Agnes landed safely on the forest floor, watching as the Arctic fox paddled to the opposite bank and dragged itself out of the water. Large clumps of its fur were missing.

Two down, she thought. *One to go.*

Leaving the fox marooned on the other side of the piranha-infested water, she collected as many fallen passion fruits as she could before sprinting back to camp. She had one last idea left, although she wasn't sure it would work.

Jabheart and Attie were still fighting when she returned.

"You've foiled me before," Jabheart snarled, thrusting a fencing sword towards Attie's throat. "You cost me that red-fanged funnel spider in Australia, but you won't meddle with my collection this time."

Attie parried the blow with his tail. "You'll never stop **SPEARS**, Jabheart!"

The third fox – dangling the disco ball in front of Elton – bared its teeth as Agnes rounded on it and began bombing it with passion fruits. They were so ripe that they exploded on impact, smothering the fox in sticky yellow seeds.

"AhooOoooOOooo!" Agnes howled as she threw. "AhooOOoo!"

The fox blinked, startled. Agnes knew she probably looked like she'd been struck with jungle fever, but she had a plan. The monkey droppings she'd spotted on the forest floor were full of passion-fruit seeds; and she knew exactly which species they belonged to.

"AhoOooOO!" she called again. These particular monkeys could smell fruit over two kilometres away; she just had to wake them up. "AhoOooO!"

She waited for a reply ... but none came. The Arctic fox grinned menacingly and turned towards her. Agnes took a step back. With a sound like a catapult launching, something rough suddenly gripped Agnes's leg and she was thrown into the air. "Whoa—!" The walls of a camouflaged net surrounded her.

It was a trap. Her chest tightened with panic. She wriggled as hard as she could, struggling to break free. Through the holes in the net she could see Attie and Jabheart sparring. Attie's tail hung low and his movements were sluggish. She wasn't sure how long he'd be able to hold Jabheart off, and she'd run out of ideas to help him.

Just then, she heard a high-pitched howl: "AhoOoO!"

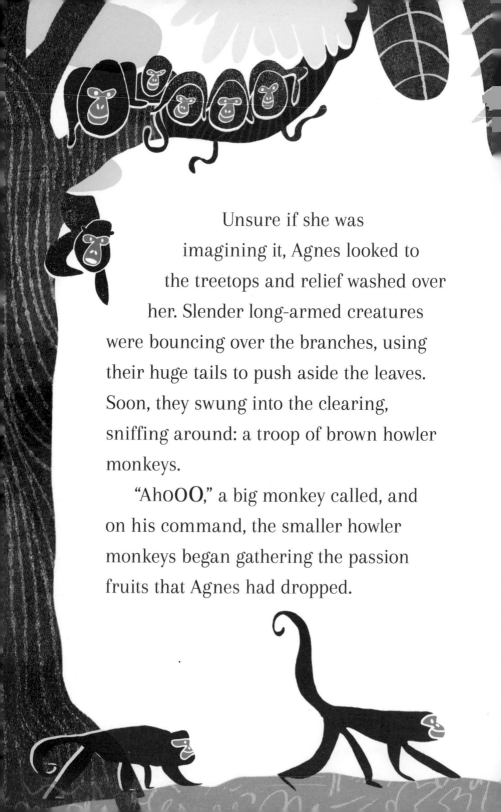

Unsure if she was
imagining it, Agnes looked to
the treetops and relief washed over
her. Slender long-armed creatures
were bouncing over the branches, using
their huge tails to push aside the leaves.
Soon, they swung into the clearing,
sniffing around: a troop of brown howler
monkeys.

"AhoOO," a big monkey called, and
on his command, the smaller howler
monkeys began gathering the passion
fruits that Agnes had dropped.

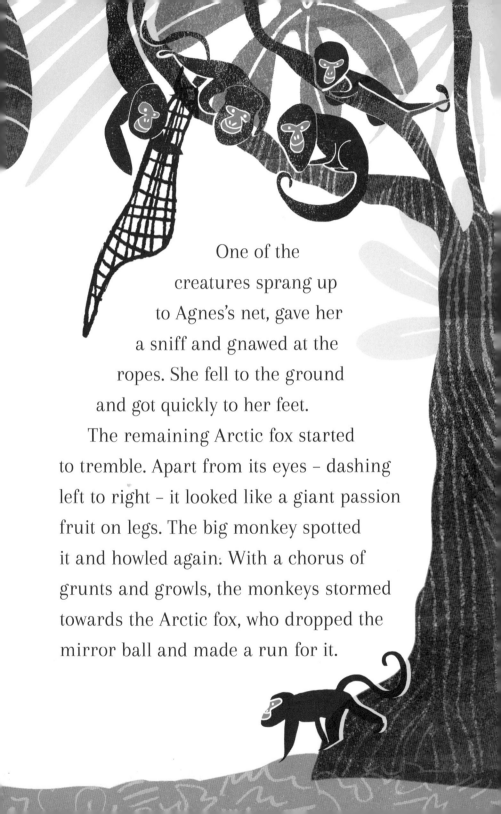

One of the
creatures sprang up
to Agnes's net, gave her
a sniff and gnawed at the
ropes. She fell to the ground
and got quickly to her feet.

The remaining Arctic fox started
to tremble. Apart from its eyes – dashing
left to right – it looked like a giant passion
fruit on legs. The big monkey spotted
it and howled again. With a chorus of
grunts and growls, the monkeys stormed
towards the Arctic fox, who dropped the
mirror ball and made a run for it.

As Agnes hurried to Elton, the monkeys lassoed the escaping Arctic fox with their tails and raised it over their heads. The fox gave a startled yelp and flattened its ears as the monkeys carried it off, picking fruit and seeds from its coat like it was their very own buffet table.

Elton's hologram blinked and swayed on the spot.

"Elton, careful!" Agnes gently scooped the bee into her hand, trying to keep him steady. "Are you OK?"

"I was having a dream about ruffles..." he mumbled.

"You had been bamboozled," Agnes explained. "Everything's all right now. You're safe." She checked on Attie, who was still using animai-tai to defend himself from Axel Jabheart's sword.

In one
swift movement,
Attie leapt into
the air and made a series
of star shapes before
landing on Jabheart's chest
and knocking him to the
floor with a loud oomph!

Jabheart's cheeks went red. "Get off me, you little rat!" he yelled, trying to swat Attie away as he got to his feet.

"I don't think so," Attie shouted defiantly. He snatched a dark green vine off the jungle floor and wrapped it around Jabheart's ankles. "Good luck trying to wriggle out of *that*. It's a strangler fig vine; impossible to break."

Elton and Agnes cheered as Jabheart fell over. After trying and failing to stand a few times, he gave up and sat with his arms folded in a huff.

"Your illegal insect-collecting days are over, Jabheart," Attie declared. He turned to Agnes. "Bring the Arctic foxes here; we'll tie them up, too."

Agnes persuaded the troop of howler monkeys to fetch the foxes, promising to give them the location of the passion-fruit vines in return.

Soon, three foxes – one patchy, one sticky and one itchy – were sitting with their tails between their legs in front of Agnes, whimpering.

"They can all stay out here overnight," Attie decided, glancing at the sky.

"Judging from those clouds, there's a rainstorm on the way."

"A rainstorm? But my suit will be ruined!" Jabheart protested. "Clam-spun sea-silk is dry-clean only!"

The sweltering Arctic foxes smiled. "Rain isss coming," they said together, sounding relieved. "Niccce coooool rain."

CHAPTER EIGHT

Emerging from the trees the next morning, Attie brushed down his **SPEARS** uniform. "The albatross glider is finally mended." There was a screwdriver poking out of his top pocket and black oil stains on his uniform. "I've put Elton inside an insect carrier to keep him safe during the journey. He'll ride inside

the glider with you. Are you ready to go?"

"I won't be a moment," Agnes said, shutting the door of Axel Jabheart's four-by-four. "I just want to see if one of these keys fits the padlock on the butterfly enclosure. I found a bunch of them on the back seat." She wiggled the first key in the lock but it wouldn't turn. "What will happen to Jabheart and the foxes?" she asked, trying another.

"I've triggered a **SPEARS** homing-beacon," Attie said. "HQ should pick up the signal and send a team out here to arrest them."

Agnes sighed with relief, glad she wouldn't be running into any of them again. Suddenly the key she was trying turned. "Got it!" The enclosure door swung open and the butterflies and other insects who had been trapped inside fluttered out.

Agnes spotted brush-footed, swallowtail and skipper butterflies among them. Their wings had so many colours and patterns Agnes felt as if she was looking through a kaleidoscope as she watched them fly away.

Once all the insects had escaped, Agnes hurried over to the take-off site and boarded the glider. Inside, she found Elton happily strapped into his insect carrier, which looked a bit like a hamster ball with a tiny chair inside.

Tufts of his velvet black fur
poked out from behind a pair
of star-shaped flight goggles.
"You look very stylish," Agnes told
him. "I'm sure you'll make a fabulous
entrance when you're reunited with
your colony."

As the glider lifted above the trees, Agnes
watched the escaped insects fly together to
spell out three words: Thank you **SPEARS**.

She waved at them out of the window, feeling proud of herself. Her parents must have had the same amazing feeling every time they had rescued a plant or animal in need. No wonder they had become **SPEARS** agents; it was the best job ever!

Agnes didn't want to think about going back to her uncle Douglas's twenty-sixth-floor flat in the big grey city. She didn't want her adventure with **SPEARS** to end. She wanted to become a permanent **SPEARS** agent, just like her mum and dad.

"You impressed me back there," Attie admitted from beside her in the cockpit. "I think you have great agent potential. But it's Commander Phil's decision in the end."

The glider veered to the right as Attie steered them out over the Paraná River.

Agnes watched the sun glittering on the surface of the water, feeling nervous. She hoped with all her might that she'd passed the field agent test.

"Our comms are back online now," Attie said. "Can you radio ahead to let them know what's happened?"

Agnes pushed a button on her headphones and spoke into the microphone. "Operation Honeyhunt has been successful!" she declared proudly. "The bee is in the honeypot. I repeat, the bee is in the honeypot. ETA at 1800 hours."

There was a crackle before Agnes heard a reply. "Received. Over."

The **SPEARS** sanctuary was hidden deep within the forest, only two hours' flight away.

Attie piloted them to a sandy clearing in the centre, which had been prepared with helipad markings. Huts with palm-thatched roofs nestled among the surrounding trees. As they flew closer, Agnes spied various animals and humans in camouflage uniform moving between them. "Do they all work for **SPEARS** too?" she asked.

Attie nodded. "Their job is to protect the sanctuary and monitor the animals living here. They'll be the ones keeping an eye on

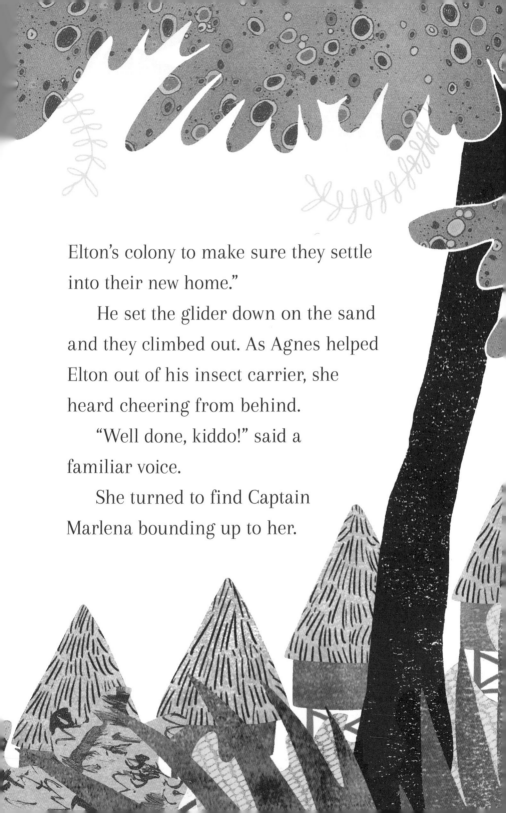

Elton's colony to make sure they settle into their new home."

He set the glider down on the sand and they climbed out. As Agnes helped Elton out of his insect carrier, she heard cheering from behind.

"Well done, kiddo!" said a familiar voice.

She turned to find Captain Marlena bounding up to her.

"Ace job in the jungle! Great agility, strength and quick-thinking."

"And first-rate flying!" added another voice. With a rustle, Aristophanes the squid emerged from the trees. He wiggled into the clearing on his tentacles and high-fived Captain Marlena. "An eye for detail, imagination and courage in abundance, I believe!"

"Oh – thank you!" Agnes said, looking rather startled. "But what are you two doing here?"

There was a low hiss and a large, hairy black-and-white ball rolled out of the sand. Agent Shadowbelly gave a long, sleepy smile. "All three of us ... are here, actually," he managed, between mouthfuls of bamboo. "And full marks ... from me, too... Determination, patience ... and cunning ... all demonstrated."

"We came to support you, of course!" Captain Marlena replied. "Commander Phil can be tough on new trainees; most don't even make it this far. We wanted to let you know that no matter what happens, you've been a star pupil and it's been a pleasure teaching you."

"And we're all rooting for you," Aristophanes added, crossing four of his arms.

Agnes smiled, although she felt tension rising in her body. If Commander Phil decided that she wasn't agent material, then her adventures with **SPEARS** would be over ... and all of this would feel like a distant dream.

Just then, Elton switched on his raindrop refractor belt and in a burst of light his hologram appeared on the sand. He stood beaming at the other agents. "Hello, everyone! Nice to meet you, I'm Elton!" He slipped his flight goggles off and replaced them with a pair of rhinestone sunglasses, before looking around. "Wow – it's beautiful here."

Agnes had to agree. She did her best to

push aside her fears about Commander Phil's upcoming decision and focus on Elton. "You must be eager to see your colony again. Come on, let's see if we can find them together."

She was about to scoop Elton into her hands when she heard a strange whirring sound, growing louder. Scanning the trees, she saw leaves rustling and parrots leaping from branches as something drew closer...

A dark cloud of bees appeared from out of the forest. They zoomed across the clearing and swarmed around Elton's hologram, buzzing excitedly.

"Lucinda! Geoffrey! Rashid...!" Elton jumped up and down, calling out an endless list of names. "I've missed you all so much. How's the new hive? Have you been dancing?"

His antennae started vibrating so fast they almost looked invisible. "Your fur is *so* shiny and I love what you've done with your wings!"

Lowering his sunglasses, he turned to Agnes and gave her the widest smile she'd ever seen him wear. "Thank you so much!"

The colony quietened as into Elton's hologram stepped another bee - this one bigger, with all-gold fur and a little crown made of tree bark.

Elton bowed. "Your *Majesty*."

The queen bee laughed and held out her front legs, pulling Elton in for a tight hug.

Happiness spread through Agnes like
warm sunshine as she watched the scene. But
it didn't last long. All of a sudden, the swarm
parted and a large black-feathered turkey
came waddling over the sand towards Agnes.
He was wearing a thick coat, woolly hat,
gloves and hiking boots.

Commander Phil wiped a wing across his brow, removing his hat and gloves. "Sorry I'm late – I've come direct from a rescue mission in the Himalayas." He removed a clipboard from under his jacket. "Now, first things first. I'm sure you're anxious to hear how I think your first mission went, Miss Gamble."

Agnes tensed. In all the excitement of Elton's family reunion, she'd almost forgotten about her assessment. She glanced at the faces of everyone gathered around her – Attie, Elton, her **SPEARS** instructors – she didn't want to let any of them down. More than that, she didn't want to let *herself* down.

Commander Phil glanced down a checklist, marking things off with a pen. He looked up at Elton. "Missing bee located and rescued," he murmured. "Rare insects freed. **SPEARS** enemies arrested..." He puffed up his chest. "Glider damaged ... overshot the landing. Got trapped in a net. Hmmm." He lifted his beak. "Before I make my final decision, I have one last challenge for you."

Agnes gave Attie a panicked look. She hadn't been told about a final challenge.

"Miss Gamble, I want you to imagine that **SPEARS** has sent you on a mission to free a humpback whale caught in a fishing net in Antarctic waters," Commander Phil said. "You can choose one **SPEARS** animal agent to accompany you. Who would it be best to take?"

Squeezing her fists, Agnes thought carefully. As a squid, Aristophanes would be the best adapted to water, although Captain Marlena might be better skilled to fight her way through a net... Eventually, Agnes reached a decision.

"The animal agent I would choose to take with me would be my partner, Agent Attenborough. It's because he and I work best as a team, no matter what the mission."

Commander Phil raised a feathery eyebrow. "I see. In that case, I have made my final decision."

The bees hummed nervously. Agnes could feel herself shaking. Had she given the right answer?

Commander Phil held out a wing towards Agnes and cleared his throat. "Congratulations, *Agent* Gamble. You have proved yourself valuable in the field and shown your understanding of **SPEARS** teamwork. I am pleased to offer you the role of permanent field agent."

Agnes's face went hot as a tingly feeling spread through her insides. "Really? I did OK?"

Commander Phil nodded, his throat wobbling. "Better than OK. I think you were exceptional. And of course, your partner gave you an excellent review."

"You did?" Agnes turned to Attie. "Oh, thank you!" Without thinking, she picked him up and hugged him tightly.

His tail twitched as he tried to wriggle free. "You're welcome, Agnes, but please put me down."

Commander Phil clapped his wings together. "That's settled then. Agent Gamble, welcome to **SPEARS**! We'll be sending you and Attie on your next mission very soon – good luck."

There was a loud hooray from the other agents, who jumped into the air, waving

their arms and tentacles. The bees swarmed
giddily about in celebration.

"I think this calls for a dance!" Elton said,
buzzing loudly. "Hive – assume positions!"

"Absolutely!" Commander Phil put his
wings in the air and shook his feathered
bottom. "Let's boogie!"

CHAPTER NINE

Sitting in her bedroom, Agnes read the postcard that Elton had sent her. On the front of it was a picture of Elton relaxing in his new hive. He was wearing bright blue sparkly sunglasses in the shape of crescent moons and drinking a glass of pink nectar that had a cocktail umbrella sticking out of the top.

In his message he'd told Agnes that although his broken leg still hadn't fully healed, he'd decided to go back to work choreographing a new dance for the bees: the shrew shuffle. Agnes was just happy that he was finally home where he belonged.

She carefully folded up her **SPEARS** uniform and slid it under her bed, wondering when she'd next have to take it out. Commander Phil had explained that she and Attie would be contacted when they were needed. In the meantime, there was always more training to do with Captain Marlena, Aristophanes and Agent Shadowbelly.

"Agnes, can you hear that purring again?" Uncle Douglas called from the hallway. "I swear that's the third time this week! I want to know where it's coming from."

Agnes jolted. "Err – it must be the neighbour's cat," she replied. "She's really loud."

Uncle Douglas grumbled, stomping back into the kitchen. "Honestly, pets should be neither seen nor heard – nor smelled, if you ask me."

Agnes chuckled to herself. Uncle Douglas knew so little about the natural world; he had no idea how loud a cat's purr really was. Besides, it wasn't a cat making that noise at all...

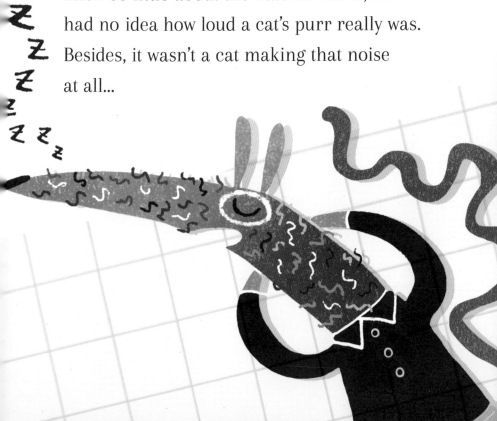

Curled up asleep, in a furry ball in the middle of Agnes's bed, was Attie. As they were off duty, he wasn't wearing his **SPEARS** uniform, which meant that if Agnes was very careful, she could stroke him.

She had discovered that whenever she did, he made a loud purring sound.

She would add it to her field notes:

ATTIE (*Rhynchocyon petersi*)
DISLIKES: Dancing, ruffles (but Elton is trying to persuade him).
LIKES: Pumpkin-seed-and-fried-banana sandwiches. AND BEING STROKED!

NOTES:
Maybe he *quite* likes human girls after all.

SPEARS HQ
FLUFFY-FACE CAT FOOD
TOWER, BIG GREY CITY

OPERATION: HONEYHUNT

MISSION TYPE:	RESCUE & RELOCATE
SPECIES NAME:	URUÇU NEGRA

MELIPONA CAPIXABA (SCIENTIFIC)

ASSIGNED EQUIPMENT:

Eco-fuel albatross glider
Raindrop refractor
Animapper

SECURITY CLASSIFICATION:

TOP SECRET

AGENT ATTENBOROUGH AND AGENT GAMBLE TO BE DEPLOYED
TO THE ATLANTIC FOREST FOR OPERATION: HONEYHUNT

CASE FILE NUMBER: 00406199602

TOP SECRET

CONFIDENTIAL

SPEARS OFFICIAL

COMMUNICATION

TOP SECRET	073
SECURITY CLASSIFICATION:	MISSION NO.

Dear Reader,

It's Commander Phil here, with very important news.

We at **SPEARS** are committed to protecting plants and wildlife under threat across the world. As you may be aware, Agents Attenborough and Gamble have recently returned from a successful operation in the Atlantic Forest, and now we need your help to continue their good work.

Do you have what it takes?

We are looking to recruit agents to carry out undercover tasks. As **SPEARS** agents, you will be required to act responsibly and show determination, quick-thinking and initiative in everyday situations.

What's the problem?

The Atlantic Forest is an incredible place that stretches across parts of Brazil, Paraguay and Argentina. It's very hot and nearly always raining, which is perfect weather for the twenty thousand species of plant and two thousand species of animal that live there. In fact, the Atlantic Forest is home to many species that can be found nowhere else on earth, which is why it's so important for us to safeguard it.

Sadly, some humans are making an elephant-dung sized mess of the whole thing. Over twenty football pitches of forest across the world are destroyed every single minute. Humans use the space for grazing cattle, growing crops, or building houses and factories. Some forest is also destroyed due to illegal logging - people cutting down trees without permission.

WHO'S IN DANGER?

Thousands of animal species live in the Atlantic Forest, from big cats like the jaguar to tiny flies like fungus gnats.

New kinds of plants and animals are still being discovered there, like the "unicorn" praying mantis, which has what looks like a horn in the middle of its head. But due to human activity like logging and farming (known as "deforestation"), many species are also in danger of extinction:

CRITICALLY ENDANGERED

GOLDEN LION TAMARIN

The Golden Lion Tamarin is a small New World monkey with awesome bright orange fur.

It sleeps in a different den each day, so predators can't find it easily.

NORTHERN MURIQUI

Known as Woolly Spider Monkeys, these are the largest monkeys in South America.

The Red-Tailed Parrot shows a band of red feathers when its tail opens.

It eats fruit, seeds, nuts and berries.

RED-TAILED PARROT

The Red-Billed
Curassow is a large,
noisy bird with black
feathers; the male
has a red bill.

CRITICALLY
ENDANGERED

RED-BILLED CURASSOW

CENTRAL HUMMING FROG

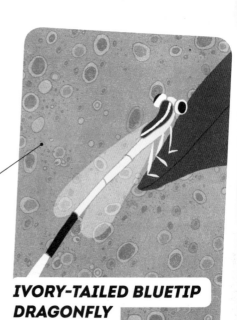

**IVORY-TAILED BLUETIP
DRAGONFLY**

The Ivory-Tailed
Bluetip Dragonfly
is VERY rare; it
has a distinctive
blue tip at the
end of its tail.

MANED THREE-TOED SLOTH

The Maned Three-Toed Sloth spends most of its life hanging upside-down in the treetops! It is the largest species of sloth.

The *Uruçu Negra* (black *Uruçu*, meaning "big bee") is so rare that it has only been found in the Brazilian state of Espirito Santo. The species of stingless bee was discovered in 1994, and added to Brazil's list of endangered species in 2003.

Only a low number of natural colonies have been discovered, which makes the species especially vulnerable to the effects of deforestation in its natural habitat.

URUCŲ NEGRA (BEE)

The *Uruçu Negra* pollinates orchids, and is a type of "eusocial" bee, which means it lives in an organized bee community in which the queen reproduces and the rest of the bees help to care for the young.

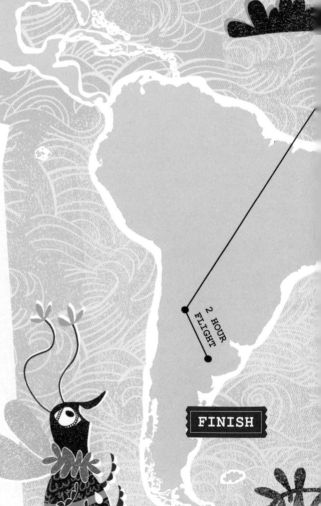

TRAVEL ROUTE

JOURNEY TO THE ATLANTIC FOREST

UNCLE DOUGLAS'S APARTMENT

THE BIG GREY CITY

SPEARS HQ

2 HOUR FLIGHT

FINISH

START

10 HOUR FLIGHT

ALBATROSS GLIDER

OPERATION: HONEYHUNT

SPEARS

AGENT GAMBLE

OPERATION: HONEYHUNT

OPERATION: HONEYHUNT

DRAGONCOPTER

THE ATLANTIC FOREST

SPEARS SANCTUARY

HOW CAN YOU HELP?

Make an eye-catching poster!

Educating people is a great way to grow their understanding of the problem of deforestation and the ways in which they can help. Your poster can include drawings and facts to illustrate what's happening in the Atlantic Forest. Talk to your friends and teachers about deforestation and its effects on animals and plants. You could even do a class project on the issue to raise awareness in your school.

SAVE OUR RAINFORESTS

Welcome bees into your garden!

Bees need looking after at home, as well as in the rainforest. Placing shallow dishes of water around your garden can help to keep bees hydrated after they've been flying around. Bees' favourite colours are blue, purple and yellow – so make sure you have lots of colourful plants and flowers in your garden to keep them happy.

Go bananas!

When you or your parents buy bananas, coffee, cocoa or tea, check that the products you choose have been certified as sustainable. This means that they are grown in a way which doesn't have a negative impact on the rainforest.

Raise money!

SPEARS isn't on its own in wanting to save the rainforest. There are some excellent organizations out there who already do good work. By doing a bake sale or hosting a school fundraiser you can donate to WWF (World Wide Fund for Nature), The Rainforest Alliance, The World Land Trust and The Nature Conservancy, among others.

Check your paper!

Paper, tissues and furniture are all made from trees. Check that any products you or your parents buy are "FSC" certified. This means they've got the stamp of approval from the Forest Stewardship Council, whose job it is to take care of forests and the people and wildlife that call them home.

Good luck. **SPEARS** is relying on you!

Sincerely,

Commander Phil

JENNIFER BELL

Londoner Jennifer Bell worked as a children's bookseller and piranha-keeper at a world-famous bookshop before becoming an author. Her debut novel, *The Uncommoners: The Crooked Sixpence* was an international bestseller. **Agents of the Wild** is her first series for younger readers. She was recruited into **SPEARS** by a giant hairy armadillo named Maurice.

ALICE LICKENS

Co-creator Alice Lickens is an illustrator and author and a winner of the prestigious Sendak Fellowship for illustration. Her picture books include *Can You Dance to the Boogaloo?*, *How To Be A Cowboy*, and the Explorer activity book series with the National Trust. She joined **SPEARS** after receiving a tap on the shoulder from a Norwegian rat named Lorita.

AGENTS OF THE WILD

OPERATION ICEBEAK